To my dearest sons, Jack and Bertie,
who are too big to carry now,
with the exception of the occasional piggyback!

First published 2023 by Walker Books Ltd
87 Vauxhall Walk, London SE11 5HJ

2 4 6 8 10 9 7 5 3 1

© 2023 Georgie Birkett

The right of Georgie Birkett to be identified as author of this work has been
asserted in accordance with the Copyright, Designs and Patents Act 1988

This book has been typeset in Butterfly Ball

Printed in China

British Library Cataloguing in Publication Data: a catalogue record
for this book is available from the British Library

ISBN 978-1-5295-0273-2

www.walker.co.uk

CHEERY
PARK

CARRY ME!
by Georgie Birkett

WALKER BOOKS
AND SUBSIDIARIES
LONDON • BOSTON • SYDNEY • AUCKLAND

When Wilbur
was very little,
his mummy loved
to sway him,

rock him,

cuddle him ...

and carry him everywhere.

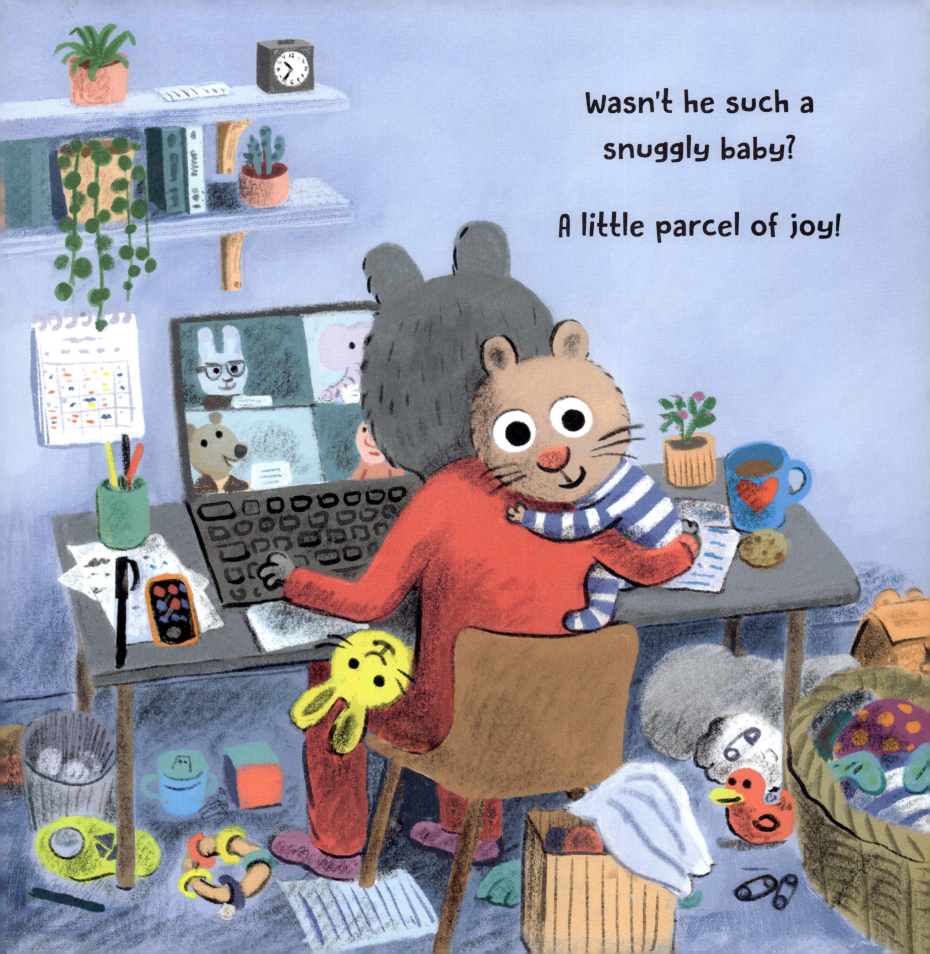

Wasn't he such a snuggly baby?

A little parcel of joy!

As wilbur got older,
he loved to do the
wiggle-waggle,

the boogie-Woogie

and shake his
little tail fluff.

He learned to do BIG jumps off benches:
"Watch this, Mummy!"

Even though Wilbur was
getting bigger and stronger,
there was ONE thing he always wanted...

"CARRY

And he really enjoyed being pushed in the buggy,
all cosy, watching the world go by.

Every day, his mummy carried and pushed him everywhere,

through rain ...

and sun ...

and snow.

But sometimes, Mummy got very tired and achy.

"Wilbur, why don't you walk home today? You're very good at walking."

Wilbur would think very hard about that.

"But my buggy will
miss me and get sad."

"My legs say,
'Not today, thank you.'"

"Actually, my shoes get
all grumpy-pumpy
when I walk."

One day, Wilbur was lazing happily in his buggy,
telling his mummy a story ...
when – oh no! – he dropped Rabbit!

Hoppity-hop,
off he went to get Rabbit.

And when he came back,
all walking on his own two feet ...

"Mummy!
You're IN my buggy!"

Well, what do you think Wilbur did next?

HE PUSHED MUMMY!
It was a bit hard work
but, oof, he pushed her ...

UP,

UUP,

UUUUP the steep hill ...

with the help of a few friends!

It's always good
to have friends to help, isn't it?
And it's always nice for mummies to have a rest, too.

After that day, Wilbur helped his Mummy and, now,
they love to walk home together,
telling each other stories.

And, actually, there is one thing Wilbur ALWAYS wants,
even more than a carry...

Can you guess what it is?

"I love you, Mummy!"

CHEERY
PARK